E
MCC   McCourt, Lisa

I love you,
Stinky Face

DUE DATE	BRODART	04/04	15.95

4/04

I Love You, Stinky Face

Written by Lisa McCourt

Illustrated by Cyd Moore

Cartwheel
·B·O·O·K·S· ®

SCHOLASTIC INC.

New York   Toronto   London   Auckland   Sydney
Mexico City   New Delhi   Hong Kong   Buenos Aires

For Aimee ~ L.M.

For my most wonderful ones,
Lindsay and Branden ~ C.M.

Text copyright © 1997 by Lisa McCourt
Illustrations copyright © 1997 by Cyd Moore

All rights reserved. Published by Scholastic Inc.
SCHOLASTIC, CARTWHEEL BOOKS, and associated logos
are trademarks and/or registered trademarks of Scholastic Inc.

Library of Congress Cataloging-in-Publication Data available

ISBN 0-439-63571-3

10 9 8 7 6 5 4 3 2 1   04 05 06 07 08

Printed in Mexico   49

First Scholastic Printing, February 2004

"I love you, my wonderful child," said Mama as she tucked me in.
But I had a question.

Mama, what if I were a **big, scary**

ape? Would you still love me then?

"If you were a big, scary ape, I would comb your whole hairy self to make sure you didn't have any tangles."

Happy Birthday! Happy

"And I would make your birthday cake out of bananas, and I would tell you, 'I love you, my big, scary ape.'"

But, Mama, but, Mama, what if I were a super smelly skunk, and I smelled so bad that my name was

Stinky Face?

"Then I would give you a bath and sprinkle you with sweet-smelling powder.

"And if you still smelled bad, I wouldn't mind, and I would hug you tight and whisper in your ear, 'I love you, Stinky Face.'"

But, Mama, but, Mama, what if I were an alligator with big, sharp teeth that could bite your head off?

"Then I would buy you a bigger toothbrush for your big teeth and make sure that you brushed them every night so they'd stay healthy and strong.

"And if you had a sore throat, I would stick my head right inside your enormous jaws to make sure you were okay, and I would say, 'I love you, my ferocious alligator.'"

But, Mama, what if I were a terrible meat-eating dinosaur with razor-sharp claws that ripped my sheets to shreds every night while I slept?

"Then I would give you plenty of meat to eat, if that is what you liked. And I would sew your sheets back together every day, because, after all, ripping them would be an accident.

"And I would tuck
you into your
newly mended
sheets every
night and say,
'I love you, my
sweet, terrible
dinosaur.'"

But, Mama, but, Mama, what if I were a swamp creature with slimy, smelly seaweed hanging from my body, and I couldn't ever leave the swamp or I would die?

"Then I would build a
house right next to the
swamp, and I would
stay with you and take
care of you always.
And when you
splashed to the
surface, I would say,
'I love you, my slimy
little swamp monster.'"

But, Mama, but, Mama, what if I were a Green Alien from Mars, and I ate bugs instead of peanut butter?

"Then I would dress you in colors that showed off your nice green skin . . .

and I would pack your lunch box with beetles and spiders and ants and grasshoppers and the tastiest bugs you ever had. And I would pack a note with all the bugs that said, 'I love you, little greenie. *Bon appétit.*'"

But, Mama, but, Mama, what if I were a **Cyclops**, and I had just one big, gigantic eye in the middle of my head?

"Then I would look right into your gigantic eye and say, 'I love you, my little cyclops,' and I would sing you a lullaby until your one gigantic eyelid got droopier and droopier, and it finally closed and you fell fast asleep."

I love you, Mama.

"And I love you, my wonderful child."